Bungalo
Books

Dedicated to the primary teachers who give children
their first gentle push toward independent reading.

Written by Frank B. Edwards
Illustrated by John Bianchi
© 1998 by Bungalo Books

First printing 1998

Cataloguing in Publication Data

Edwards, Frank B., 1952-
New at the zoo

(Bungalo Books new reader series)
ISBN 0-921285-70-1 (bound)　　　ISBN 0-921285-69-8 (pbk.)

I. Bianchi, John　　II. Title.　　III. Title: Series

PS8559.D84N48 1998　　jC813'.54　　C97-901181-7
PZ7.E2535Ne 1998

Published in Canada by:
Bungalo Books
Ste.100
17 Elk Court
Kingston, Ontario
K7M 7A4

Trade Distribution:
Firefly Books Ltd.
3680 Victoria Park Ave.
Willowdale, Ontario
M2H 3K1

Co-published in U.S.A. by:
Firefly Books (U.S.) Inc.
Ellicott Station
P.O. Box 1338
Buffalo, New York
14205

Printed in Canada by:
Friesen Printers
Altona, Manitoba
ROG OBO

Visit Bungalo Books on the Net at:
www.BungaloBooks.com

Send E-mail to Bungalo Books at:
Bungalo@cgocable.net

New
at the Zoo

Written by Frank B. Edwards
Illustrated by John Bianchi

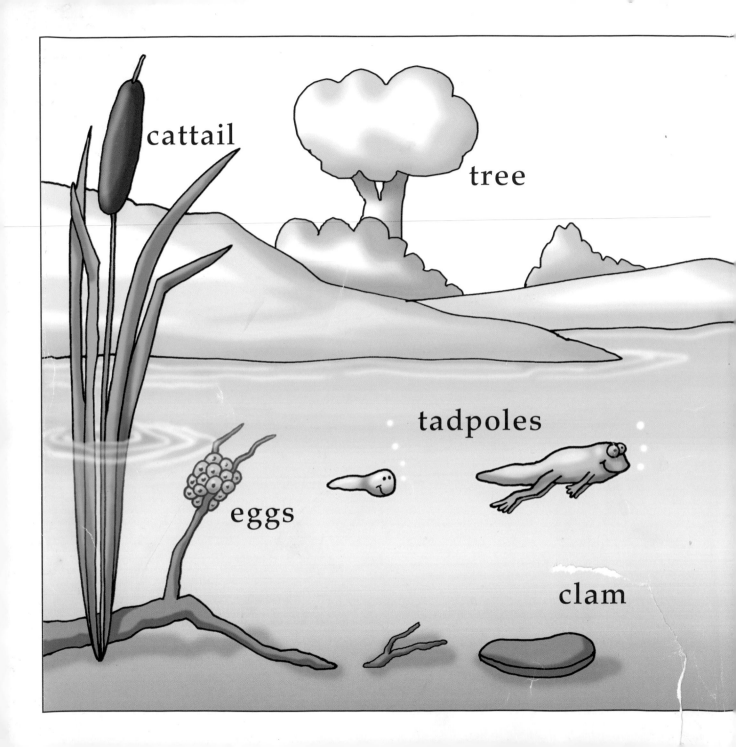

I am new. May I play with you?

Not now. I am going to a party.

I am new.
May I play with you?

Not now. We are going to a party.

I am new. May I play with you?

Not now.
We are going to a party.

I am new. May I play with you?

Not now. We are going to a party.

Come with me to a party
for our new friend.

Who is your new friend?

Our new friend is you!

The End